DATE DUE

Peter's Trucks

ALBERT WHITMAN & COMPANY • Morton Grove, Illinois

Sallie Wolf • Illustrated by Cat Bowman Smith

With love to Lou and Peter and Chuck,
and to Peter Frostic, who saw the first truck. S.W.

To my son Alex. C.B.S.

The illustrations were done in ink and watercolor.
The typeface is ITC Benguiat Gothic Bold.
Typography by Karen Johnson Campbell.

Library of Congress Cataloging-in-Publication Data
Wolf, Sallie.
Peter's trucks / Sallie Wolf; illustrated
by Cat Bowman Smith.
p. cm.
Summary: A boy sees many different types
of trucks and learns what each one carries.
ISBN 0-8075-6519-9
[1. Trucks—Fiction. 2. Stories in rhyme.]
I. Smith, Cat Bowman, ill. II. Title.
PZ8.3.W8425Pe 1992   91-19251
[E]—dc20   CIP
                                    AC

Text © 1992 by Sallie Wolf.
Illustrations © 1992 by Cat Bowman Smith.
Published in 1992 by Albert Whitman & Company,
6340 Oakton Street, Morton Grove, Illinois 60053-2723.
Published simultaneously in Canada by
General Publishing, Limited, Toronto.
10 9 8 7 6 5 4 3 2 1

There are all kinds of trucks, as everyone knows.
Peter finds trucks wherever he goes.

A blue and red truck at the grocery store
with a painted cow on the back of the door.
"Mister, mister, are there cows in your truck?"
"No cows, sonny, just milk."

A big, gray truck rolls up to the pumps.
The driver looks out, then down he jumps.
"Mister, mister, is there milk in your truck?"
"No milk, Mac, just gas."

A long, green truck—on the side there's a name.
Peter looks up from playing his game.
"Mister, mister, is there gas in your truck?"
"No gas, kiddo, just a piano."

Rattling, roaring, binging, banging,
here comes a truck with a loud, proud clanging.
"Mister, mister—oops!
Lady, lady, is there a piano in your truck?"
"No piano, bambino, just garbage."

Ringing and dinging and singing its song,
a musical white and brown truck rolls along.
"Mister, mister, is there garbage in your truck?"
"No garbage, little guy, just ice cream.
Want to buy?"

A short, squat truck drives up to the bank.
The first guard out gives the door a yank.
A second leaps down from the truck with a sack
and runs to the bank with the sack on her back.
"Lady, lady, is there ice cream in your truck?"
"No ice cream, honey, just money."

A heavy truck, a yellow truck,
a rumbling, grumbling, grinding truck.
Round and round turns the back of this truck.
Then it stops. There's a whoosh and a swoosh and a toot.
What's that slithering down the chute?
"Mister, mister, is there money in your truck?"
"No such luck, Chuck, just concrete."

A muddy truck on a country road,
lumbering slowly with its heavy load.
It rolls to a stop in front of a barn.
Forget the cucumbers. Forget the fresh corn.
Follow that truck!

"Mister, mister, is there concrete in your truck?"
"No, no concrete, sonny."
"How about money?"
"No such luck, Chuck."
"You wouldn't have ice cream?"
"Nice try, little guy."
"I see lots of flies. Is there garbage inside?"
"I should say not. The flies come for the ride."
"How about a piano?"
"No piano, bambino."
"Is gas your cargo?"
"No gas, kiddo."
"Is there milk in the back?"
"No milk, Mac."
"Mister, mister, please—
What *is* in your truck?"
"Take a look now."

"Wow! Cows!"